Endorsements

In the finest traditions of Christian children's literature, Mike and Carol Wyrick have penned another classic. The trying circumstances of life, including disabilities, can seem overwhelming. But God has a purpose for each of us, and we find meaning and hope by trusting God. That is the vital message of *A Miracle for Micah*, which beautifully weaves biblical truths into a captivating story set in the Palestine of Jesus' earthly ministry. This outstanding book, with very contemporary and relevant themes, is destined to build knowledge, character, and hope in young readers. One of the best children's books I have read. I highly recommend *A Miracle for Micah!*

—**Mark Presson**
Vice President, Administration and Finance
Emmaus Bible College
Dubuque, Iowa

A Miracle for Micah is a wonderful story for children and adults. We learn about God's unconditional love for each of us. Micah's parents, family, and friends had their doubts, but in spite of seemingly insurmountable challenges, they learned that God has a plan and meaningful purpose for all of our lives. The story provides great insight regarding people with disabilities and helps us understand that God wants us to love, respect, and accept each other. Micah teaches also that young disabled people are the same as their friends and classmates. They want to be loved and have the opportunity to learn, achieve, work, and be a contributing member of their community. Micah's family and friends develop a renewed faith in God and learn the value of loving and supporting their neighbors—a message as important today as it was 2,000 years ago.

—**Jeffrey W. Cooper**
President/CEO
United Cerebral Palsy of Central Pennsylvania
Camp Hill, Pennsylvania

This story is written for every family member. The heart of this timely message should be read and reread among all age groups, never to be forgotten. It is useful in counseling children, both individually and in groups. I have been working with families for over thirty years, and wish I had had this book when I first began.

—**Jerome Shapiro, Ph.D.**
Counseling Psychologist and Educator
Ashburn, Virginia

This wonderful and poignant story teaches hope, faith, perseverance, sensitivity, and God's greatest commandments—love him and love one's neighbors. It teaches, too, that God has a special plan for each one of us. This message is critical for individuals, families, teachers, counselors, pastors, and community leaders.

With daily media attention to incidents of intimidation, bullying, exclusion, and continued discrimination, we all must continually examine our own sensitivities. Characters in this story model how we can lead, cooperate with, and encourage one another in the best and most challenging of times.

—Frederick A. Vago
President, Danya International, Inc.
"Innovative Solutions for Social Impact"
Silver Spring, Maryland

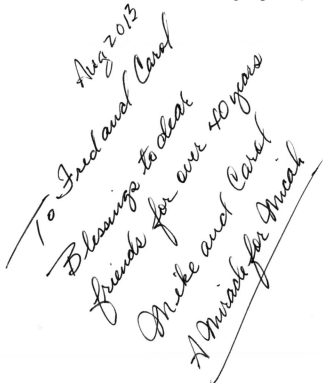

Aug 2013

To Fred and Carol
Blessings to dear
friends for over 40 years
Mike and Carol
A Miracle for Micah

A Miracle
For
Micah

A MIRACLE FOR MICAH

FAITH IN HARD TIMES

MIKE AND CAROL WYRICK
ILLUSTRATED BY DAVID MILES

WinePress **Kids**
Great Books, Defined.

CONTENTS

LETTER FROM THE AUTHORS
TO PARENTS, EDUCATORS, HOMESCHOOL TEACHERS, PASTORS, AND SMALL-GROUP LEADERS

YOUNG PEOPLE ARE often acquainted with the familiar Bible stories of Adam, Noah, Moses, David, and the birth and life of Jesus. But there are many other Bible characters not as well known whose stories offer hope and faith to today's young people.

It is fun for young people to imagine Bible stories and their lessons through their own eyes. As they envision the many daily, unrecorded activities that climax in biblical events, they often see how their own lives are developing as part of God's plan. They can glean biblical guidance as well as discuss their thoughts with friends, family, and teachers. In the same way, readers will encounter situations and events in *A Miracle for Micah* that will allow them to examine their faith in God and learn how he can work in their own lives. Some of these include:

- A young person encounters a situation that makes him angry at God.

- A family examines why bad things happen and how they, as believers, should respond.
- Young people in a community realize their shortcomings and create an opportunity to help a friend.
- An entire community unites around a selfless purpose.
- People learn what it means to "love the Lord your God with all your heart and with all your soul and with all your mind," and to "love your neighbor as yourself" (Matthew 22:37,39).
- A family and community witness the power of faith. "Everything is possible for him who believes" (Mark 9:23).

A discussion guide is included at the end of the book for use by parents, educators, homeschool teachers, pastors, and small-group leaders. We hope this guide will encourage group discussion and help young people share their thoughts about the story with others.

CHAPTER 1

ESCAPE

K EEP GOING, KEEP going," young Reuben groaned to himself through gritted teeth. He pulled himself along on his stomach through the mud on the dark, narrow road leading out of the village. The freezing, nighttime rain drizzled down on him. His tunic was soaked and torn. His legs and bare feet dragged along behind him. *Useless things,* he thought. *I'll be glad when my miserable life is over.*

Reuben knew he had to hurry if he wanted to escape. His mother and father would be looking for him once they found he was gone from his bed. By that time, he hoped to be floating lifelessly in the Sea of Galilee.

He never realized when he fell asleep from exhaustion, nor did he feel the strong hands that gripped his arms and lifted him out of the mud.

He awoke in a tiny room dimly lit by two candles. There was a fire in an earthen fireplace, which was common to the mud brick houses in the village. Reuben realized someone had cleaned him up and changed his clothes. The bed in which he lay was not much more comfortable than his bed at home, but it felt good to be warm and dry. *Where am I? How did I get here?* he wondered as he struggled to sit up.

A bearded man in a dark brown robe sat in a wooden chair facing the fireplace, slowly drinking from a stone cup. His back was to Reuben. He turned when he heard the boy rustle on the bed. "Ah," he said, "you're awake now. How do you feel?"

Reuben ignored the question. "Where am I?" he asked.

"You're with friends," the man replied. "We found you around midnight. Good thing we did, too. You would have soon drowned in the mud or frozen to death. How did you get there? You don't look like the type who would want to be outside at all, much less where you were."

"I had my reasons," Reuben answered. "I wish you had left me there. I wanted to die."

"Why would a young person your age want to die?" asked the man.

"Since you carried me, you probably didn't notice that I am unable to walk."

"Then how did you get there?"

"I got there by pulling myself with my arms."

"Where do you live?"

"I live with my parents in the village."

"Where are they now?"

Reuben sighed. "Surely they are looking for me. I was hoping to be dead by the time they got up this morning."

The man handed Reuben a cup, which warmed his hands. "Here is some broth for you to drink," he said. "Soon we will have bread and lamb, which the villagers have brought me."

"Who are you?" asked Reuben.

"I'm just a simple priest. I and a few others have a small church and are followers of Jesus Christ. I'm sure you've heard of him."

Reuben had heard the name Jesus before. Jesus had lived more than thirty years ago. But Reuben had heard more about Jews and Romans. The Romans had conquered Israel more than one hundred years ago, and the Jews were under their control. Ironically, though, both the Jewish priests and the Roman soldiers harassed Reuben's parents for keeping a disabled boy at home when there were other places "such people" should go.

"Again, why would you want to die?" asked the man.

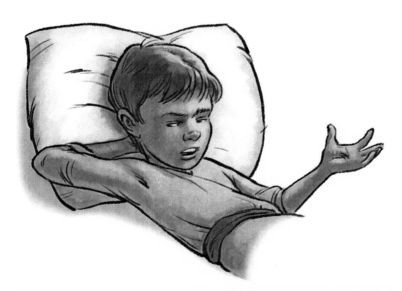

"Everyone knows the burden of a disabled person," said Reuben. "Our conditions can't be cured. We are isolated, either by laws or by so-called friends and neighbors. We are often accused of being the product of sin—either our own or that of our parents. I see the hardship I cause my family, and I am constantly miserable. I have never known a happy moment except when I was very young. Little children often don't notice differences in people until they are older. But now that I am a teenager, I have no friends. I have no future, and I want my misery to be over."

The man sat silently and sipped his broth. He occasionally stirred the tiny fire and added sticks to keep it going. "You describe a very grim situation," he said.

"Grim situation! I'm worse than a dead person!" Reuben blurted out. "What do you know?" He turned away as his anger brought tears to his eyes.

"I've heard this story so many times," said the man. "Yours is no different."

"How could you have heard this story so many times?" Reuben turned his face in the man's direction.

"People come to our little church when they face hard times. They have lost their faith, and with it they've lost their hope. They often think death is the only solution."

"Well, what solution do you have to offer?"

"It's not what solution we have to offer, it's what solution God has to offer. We just try to keep people from denying God his will, such as you would have done if we hadn't found you."

"Why does God create people like me?" Reuben asked, staring up at the ceiling. "What future could I have? Why do I and the people who love me have to suffer?"

The man leaned toward him. "God created you. He created you for his purpose, not yours. He knows your pain. Think about this: perhaps the pain causes you and those around you to focus on God. Your anger and sadness cause you to focus on him in a

4

way you otherwise might not. You can't take God for granted. There are benefits to all this that I can see that you can't, because you are so young and in so much pain."

Reuben looked back toward the man. "Tell me one benefit."

"The love of your parents," the man said without hesitation. "You told me that right now they are looking for you. Would they be if you were such a burden to them? Isn't it out of love that they are doing that?"

"Well, then, tell me what purpose God might have for me. I can see the purpose for the children in the village who are physically able, but I can't see mine."

"I don't know what God has in mind for you. I can't say it for anyone. We all must be patient, and maybe wait an entire lifetime. We may never fully understand how God will use us. It may come in many little things we do throughout our lives that affect others in ways we don't even know. Also, God has us working with each other to achieve his purpose. Keep in mind that he created you as a unique individual and loves you as much as he does anyone else. But you must have faith. That is the most important thing."

"You say you have many stories," said Reuben. "Will you share one with me?"

The man sat back in his chair. He took another sip from his cup and stared into the tiny fire. "I will," he said. "I'll tell you the story of a miracle for Micah."

CHAPTER 2

FROM WARRIORS
HE CAME

REUBEN NOTICED THE man's eyes glistened as he spoke. Occasionally, he would move his hands as he described a memory he was bringing back to life. Reuben yawned and strained to pay attention.

"Israel has been governed by the Roman Empire for more than one hundred years. The Romans are brutal in using fear, torture, and crucifixion to keep people in line. They take land from farmers and steal from merchants. Often, they burn crops and kill livestock simply out of meanness. They believe in false gods and torment the Jews because of their faith. Jews are killed every day for their beliefs. Life is terrible for everyone in Israel.

"There is little the Jews can do to fight the powerful Roman army. However, for many years there has been a secret Jewish army known as the Zealots. These are men who come from villages and the countryside to form small raiding parties. They operate at night, staging hit-and-run attacks on Roman outposts. Then they escape back to their homes or caves in the hills.

"Their most daring missions are assassinations of Roman leaders who appear in public. These involve the boldest Zealots known as 'dagger men.' They carry long knives inside their robes. In plain daylight, they move among the crowds toward their victims. With lightning speed, they stab them to death, and as the crowd panics, they escape among the people. The Romans execute many innocent Jews in search of these murderers.

"Roman soldiers have orders to capture and kill Zealots on sight. They race from village to village ransacking homes and torturing old men and women to find even one Zealot. Zealots rarely gather in one spot, but occasionally a few are cornered and fight to the death. One famous story involves a group of Roman soldiers who captured a notorious Zealot leader in a hillside hideout. They executed him in front of his whole family and quickly spread the word to all the Jewish communities.

"Years ago, in this very village, lived a strong, handsome man named Caleb. He had been popular since childhood and was a natural leader. His father and grandfather were successful fishermen, and Caleb was destined to take over their trade. Life for him seemed perfect.

"But Caleb was never satisfied. Those who knew him best say he was cut out for something more adventurous. He left his village when he was only eighteen to learn better fishing methods on the Mediterranean Sea, far to the west. However, it was whispered that he was actually on secret missions as the captain of a Zealot group.

"The rumors about Caleb made everyone love and respect him even more. Daring stories about him were told around every shepherd's campfire and at every family's dinner table. A favorite one was that he had led a band of horsemen on a raid against a heavily-armed Roman supply caravan. More than thirty

Romans had been killed, but only two Zealots were lost. Caleb became a legend.

"One stormy night, Caleb returned back home. His right shoulder and upper arm had been seriously injured. It must have been a wound from a Roman sword. He struggled to the little house of one of his brothers named Benjamin. Benjamin took him in and, with the help of all the villagers, kept his presence a secret for many days. Eventually, additional help was needed. Benjamin had to return to his fishing business and could no longer tend to Caleb's needs.

"In the village lived a beautiful young Jewish woman named Naomi. She had recently moved from the countryside to live with friends. She, too, had a mysterious past. Her father, mother, and brothers had not come with her. No one knew exactly what had happened to them, but rumors were that they had also been Zealots and had been killed by the Romans. No one wanted to know for sure. The threat of torture and questioning by the Romans was too strong.

"Benjamin called for Naomi to come to his house. Caleb's life was no longer in danger because of his injury, but it was clear he needed someone to nurse him back to health. Naomi agreed to care for him.

"Over the next several weeks, Caleb and Naomi found they had many things in common. They loved God, they were devout Jews, they hated the Romans, and they admired the efforts of the Zealots.

"As Caleb recovered, he rejoined the normal activities of the community. He and Naomi were seen throughout the village. It was soon announced they had fallen in love and would be married.

"Caleb and Naomi were married in a traditional Jewish wedding. The whole village enjoyed a festive, seven-day celebration.

The only sadness the couple felt was that Naomi's family was not there to participate.

"After the marriage, Caleb took a position on the village council and began fishing again with his brothers on the Sea of Galilee. But they knew he was not happy. His warrior heart was still in fighting the Romans, but that was no longer possible due to his injury. However, he had a secret dream.

"Each evening, Caleb and Naomi talked about their faith. They appreciated their life together and the many blessings God had given them. Then Caleb shared his dream with her.

"'This war to overthrow the Romans will go on for years,' he said. 'I can't fight anymore. But it's important there be warriors who can.' Naomi listened closely.

"'If we were to have a son, hopefully he would inherit our families' abilities. He could carry on the fight and be a famous warrior like those in Jewish history. Then your father and brothers would not have died in vain. A strong warrior would be a legacy for everyone.'

"Naomi was inspired. She prayed every night that Caleb's dream would come true. She thought about heroes in Scripture such as Abraham and Sarah, who prayed that they would be blessed with a son. She thought of the mother of the prophet Samuel, who told God that if she were blessed with a son, she would give the boy back to him for the priesthood.

"God heard Naomi's prayers. After anxiously waiting, she became pregnant. The family was filled with joy. Caleb could not wait until the child's birth. But then, an unimaginable tragedy struck."

CHAPTER 3

TERRIBLE AND UNFAIR

BEFORE CALEB COULD see his child, he died. His old injury had weakened him, and the cold, rainy winter typical of Galilee caused him to get pneumonia. Naomi and Caleb's father and brothers prayed for him, but with all of them gathered around him, Caleb breathed his last breath. The family was devastated. They had lost their son, brother, husband, and soon-to-be father. The village had lost a heroic leader and friend.

"Naomi was overcome with grief. She was now a widow, and being a young, single woman with a new child had serious social challenges. She had few ways to support herself. She was largely dependent upon whatever support Caleb's family could give her.

"On the day of the child's birth, dark, low-hanging clouds filled the sky, and cold rain poured down. The women of the village surrounded Naomi as she struggled through the birth.

Soon, the tiny cries of a baby boy brought tears of joy to everyone's eyes. Naomi named him Micah, meaning 'prophet.'

"Naomi praised God as she gazed into the face of her newborn son. The family passed him from one set of open arms to another, singing and praying over him. His birth made Naomi feel as if Caleb's spirit was present in the dimly-lit room.

"However, the women soon realized that something was wrong. Micah couldn't move his legs. The women tickled his feet to see if he would respond. Sadly, it seemed that Micah had no feeling in his legs at all. He was the happiest of babies, but he would never be able to walk.

"Naomi was heartbroken. Caleb's dream had been for Micah to be a warrior. 'What have I done to deserve this?' she cried out to God. 'My husband, mother, father, and brothers died for you. We have been totally faithful. If Caleb were here, he would be devastated.'

"Naomi now faced a more serious problem. A disabled child might have a bleak future. If he could not work, he couldn't help support the family. If his family couldn't support him, his only hope would be to beg. As he grew older, Micah's problems would only get worse. He might eventually be an outcast from the village.

"Naomi prayed for many days, but she felt she heard no response from God. She lay in bed and spoke to no one.

"Caleb's family also felt that God had dealt them a terrible and unfair blow. Life in a tiny village was unbelievably hard. Every person had to do his or her part, from fishing to cooking to caring for family members. 'Why did this happen?' the family demanded. Their emotions ranged from sadness to anger at God.

"Micah's grandfather called them all together to talk about the situation and pray for God's guidance. Daniel, Caleb's youngest brother, stood to speak. 'God has been good to our family,' he said. 'But we have shown plenty of appreciation. We have thanked him every day of our lives. Scriptures, prayer, and his teachings have been a major part of our family's life. God has been unfair.'

"'Think about the story of Job,' Joshua, the middle brother, argued back. 'Job is a hero of the Scriptures. He lost his entire family and all his wealth. But he had faith in God, and all that he had lost was restored. We must remain steadfast!'

"Benjamin agreed. 'How are we any different than Joseph or Moses? God was with them through terrible times and rewarded their faith by making them some of the greatest heroes in history.'

"The meetings continued for several evenings until Grandfather gathered them around to have the final say. 'I have listened to each of you,' he said. 'We have all been affected by Micah's condition. We wonder why God would let this happen. Even more serious, some of us are angry with him.'

"'I have searched the Scriptures, and I believe the answer is clear. God says to trust in him. We feel sorry for ourselves. But why? We have had many blessings. I think God is testing us the way Job was tested. So, let us renew our faith in God and do what he would have us do—support Naomi and Micah—and see what his will brings.'

"The following evening, Grandfather and his three sons gathered around Naomi. 'Naomi,' he said, 'we have come to confess our shame and disappointment in ourselves. We love you and little Micah. You are both a big part of our lives. You are God's blessings to us. We are sorry about Micah's condition. We know how much you and Caleb prayed for a strong son. Your hope, and ours, was that he would be a warrior like his father. Together we have prayed, but now we realize we have been selfish. We have been happy only as long as everything has gone our way. It may be that we have loved ourselves first and God second. We have sinned in letting our own personal desires come before your needs.

"'We feel God has given us a second chance. He has called us to provide the love and support you and little Micah need. We know your fears, but you should put them all aside. Together, we will raise Micah to do what God has planned for him.'

"Naomi could hardly respond. She was overcome by grief.

"As the years passed, the family adjusted to the challenge. They developed a plan for Micah's growth in spite of the obstacles society put before him. Grandfather and his uncles taught him the Scriptures and gave him simple chores. They entertained him with stories of the Zealots, of fishing adventures, and of heroes in Jewish history. Naomi tended to his daily needs.

"Nonetheless, the powerful and unforgiving priests harassed Naomi when she went to the market. They told her that her anger with God over Caleb's death had caused Micah's problems. Neighbors said hidden sins had brought God's punishment.

Micah was not even allowed to attend the teachings of the local rabbi. Children would not play with him. Some taunted him and called him names that hurt Micah so badly he never wanted to go outside.

"As he grew to be a teenager, he developed emotional problems. He became depressed about his future. His loneliness grew more painful. Naomi began to find it difficult to reason with him. Each night, she pleaded, 'Micah, you must not lose faith. We must pray to God about this.'

"One evening, Micah sinned greatly. His misery was overwhelming, and he cried out, 'I hate God! There is no God!' Naomi was terrified. She stood over him and begged him not to say such things. Micah had committed the worst of sins by denying God's existence.

"'Mother, if you truly loved me, you would have let me die!' Micah cried.

"Naomi wept. 'Remember,' she said, 'God has a plan for you!'

"'Why would God plan this for someone he created?' Micah angrily replied. 'I do not believe in him.'

"Naomi cried in desperation. What could she do now? She needed a miracle."

CHAPTER 4

THE BLESSING OF YOUNG PEOPLE

CAPERNAUM HAD BEEN blessed with a large group of young people, from infants to teenagers. This meant the future of the village was secure. As the parents aged, their children would take over family trades and businesses.

"The youngsters were like those in all villages. They were energetic, played games, made close friendships, and had their leaders and followers. Most of the leaders were positive, healthy, and smart. They led wholesome activities, and their friends adopted their attitudes and wanted to be a part of everything they did. But some of the leaders were bullies, and their followers were the same. They disrupted village activities and threatened many of the other kids.

"In either case, the leaders influenced the thinking of others. They modeled behavior. If they liked or disliked someone or some activity, they could influence others to do the same.

"Some kids were always left out. These were usually the ones who were somehow different. Perhaps they looked different from the other kids. Maybe they dressed differently or came from families in which there were difficulties. For whatever reason, they were simply left out.

"One boy named Ariel was a popular leader. He was big, strong, and smart. He was kind to everyone, behaved well, and participated in all the village activities. All the young people wanted to be like him. If Ariel liked something or someone, his followers did as well.

"Micah had cousins who were popular. Often, their friends came around his home. Whenever they saw him, they hardly knew what to do or say. Often they said nothing, even though he was right there in front of them. They never asked him if he wanted to join in what they were doing. Occasionally, they made hateful remarks. While they rarely said them loudly, he would often hear them. Micah was different, and, as a result, he was simply left out.

"Micah's mind was as clear as theirs. His body was disabled, but his mind was not. He often wondered, *Why don't the others ask me to come outside? Am I so different that I can't even join in their conversation? Does my physical appearance make them feel that uneasy? Even worse, why don't my own cousins invite me out? At home we get along fine, but around their friends they ignore me. Are they ashamed of me?*

"Micah decided to take the problem to his family and ask for guidance."

CHAPTER 5

A FAMILY'S WISDOM

M ICAH LOVED HIS grandfather and uncles. Each
night after dinner, they would tell him stories of the
heroes of the Scriptures. The stories would always lead to lengthy
discussions.

"One evening, Micah asked his family for advice. 'I worry
about my future,' he said. 'Other kids will grow up and take
over their families' trades. I'm not going to be able to do that.
I have no friends. The kids my age avoid me. The leader of the
local kids stares at me. I don't know what he is thinking, but
what he says and does, the others do as well. I'm afraid of him.
I will have to deal with this all my life.'

"'Micah, you may be imagining this,' said Benjamin. 'But
I'm curious. Who is this leader?'

"'His name is Ariel,' said Micah.

"The uncles glanced at one another. They were puzzled by
Micah's response.

"'This is an important matter,' Daniel said. 'Let us think about this, and we'll discuss it more tomorrow.'

"The next day, the uncles talked about the previous night's conversation and Micah's remark about Ariel. 'Could this Ariel, the leader Micah says he is afraid of, be the boy who works with us in our fishing business?' Benjamin asked. 'Surely, this can't be the same person.'

"'Ariel is a great kid,' said Daniel. 'He's kind, respectful, and works hard. Everyone enjoys being around him. He may simply not know how to relate to a disabled person. Micah may misinterpret his staring at him.'

"They agreed this must be a misunderstanding. 'Micah might be disabled,' said Daniel, 'but mentally, he is as sharp as Ariel. We know them both. I think the two just need to get to know one another.'

"Benjamin had an idea. 'I don't know why I never thought of this before,' he said. 'Why don't we let Micah come work with us in our fishing business? Without strong legs, he can't go out on the boats. But his hands and arms are strong. He can stay on our docks and mend the nets. We could use his help, and this way he could get to know Ariel.'

"The men agreed. In the following days, Micah learned how to mend the nets. Each morning, his uncles carried him to the docks, where he sat on a cushion under an awning. Micah mended the nets where they had become damaged. He enjoyed being outside, talking with the fishermen, and watching the boats go out onto the Sea of Galilee. At night, he liked to share fishing stories with his uncles as they ate dinner.

"Micah's relationship with Ariel began slowly. At first, Ariel was curious about how Micah had become involved in the fishing business at all. But they were very busy, and he couldn't pay much attention to Micah. Nonetheless, it was difficult for the two to avoid one another. They both mended nets when the wind was too strong for the boats to leave the docks. Conversation was difficult, for they shared little in common. But as they worked together on many tasks, their comfort with one another grew.

"One day, a huge, towering thunderstorm threatened on the far side of the lake. A ferocious wind roared in suddenly. Micah's uncles moved quickly to tie up their boats and those of their neighbors on the docks down the shore. Ariel was left to help Micah fold the nets so they could be secured on the beach. Black clouds were on top of them within minutes. Driving rain separated Micah and Ariel from the uncles. Both heaved the nets into wet piles. Ariel began dragging them off the dock and as far up the beach as he could so the ever-growing waves couldn't wash them away.

"Micah was still out on the far end of the dock. The thunder and lightning were frightening. The dock was being destroyed.

Boards began to crack under the pounding waves and fly away in the ferocious wind. Without strong legs, Micah couldn't escape. Within minutes, he would be totally stranded and at the mercy of the storm.

"Ariel realized Micah was in grave danger. For the first time in his life, he felt he might not be able to help. He yelled for the uncles, but they were too far away helping other fishermen. There was no way for them to hear him. The rain was pounding heavier, and huge, dark swells of water were rolling toward the docks.

"Ariel did the only thing he could do. He carefully made his way back out on the dock toward Micah. He could see the water beneath him where the wooden planks had been ripped from the dock. Finally, he reached Micah, who sat frozen in fear. Ariel lifted him into his arms and moved carefully back toward the beach. He leaned into the wind and staggered to keep his balance. He knew that if they fell into the water, they would surely drown. Micah wrapped his arms around Ariel's neck and prayed they would make it to safety before the whole dock gave way.

"Once they reached the beach, Ariel fell forward onto his knees. Micah rolled onto the sand in front of him. The two saw an open storage shed used for nets and scrambled to what they hoped would be safety. Ariel noticed that Micah could crawl almost as fast as he could.

"After an hour, the storm left as quickly as it had come. Within minutes, Micah's uncles threw open the door to the storage shed. Inside, they found Micah and Ariel, soaking wet and covered with sand and seaweed. They looked at one another, relieved that the boys had escaped the terrible storm.

"Ariel patted Micah on the shoulder. 'Hey, Micah!' he said. 'You're heavier than I thought you'd be.'

"'And faster, too,' said Micah. Everyone laughed.

"The storm turned out to be a blessing, as it created a bond between two unlikely friends. Who knew this friendship would soon spark ideas for projects that would have lifelong impact?"

CHAPTER 6

ARIEL'S GREAT IDEA

THE NEXT DAY, the kids from the village sat under a shade tree eating pomegranates and talking about the storm. They were excited as they discussed how fast it had come up. Each had a story of where he or she had been when the storm hit and what he or she had been doing. Everyone grew quiet when Ariel told his story. He spoke of how he and Micah had escaped the collapsing dock and stayed in the storage shed until Micah's uncles came to get them. The others were fascinated by his tale.

"'That must've been fun,' said one boy sarcastically.

"'Hey, Micah's a cool kid!' Ariel said. 'Even during the storm, he insisted we take care of the nets before we thought of ourselves. He knows how valuable they are to his family and the entire village. We barely escaped with our lives, but Micah hung in there every minute. And, to tell you the truth, when we hit the beach, I could hardly keep up with him as we crawled across the sand. I guess thunder and lightning can do that to a person.' Everyone laughed.

"'Micah is a great worker,' Ariel continued. 'I know I can count on him, and he's got a great sense of humor. I really like working with him.'

"He paused for a moment. 'I've got an idea. Why don't we all get involved with the fishing business? We can mend nets, work the boat ropes, unload fish, and do other things. I know we have family chores and our fathers' trades to learn, but this could be something fun for us to do in our spare time. We spend hours playing games and just hanging out. We could be doing something more productive. It would allow us to really get to know each other and help the village at the same time.'

"Everyone looked at each other, and then nodded their heads in agreement.

"'How do we get started?' one boy asked.

"'I'll talk to Micah's uncles and find out what we can do,' Ariel replied.

"The following week, Ariel asked Benjamin if he would present the idea to the other fishermen in the village. Benjamin agreed. Everyone liked the idea. After all, who could argue against extra help? The uncles knew that allowing the young people to work at whatever they could do would be fun. Furthermore, it would help them develop into future leaders.

"Ariel worked with Micah's uncles to organize the project. The fishermen would teach the activities, the women would bring food and water to the docks each day, and the kids with experience would teach the others.

"This was Micah's chance to fit in. He knew how to mend the nets. Tie one knot here; loop the material there. Keep working until the yards of nets were free of rips, tangles, or tiny fish too small to keep.

"Micah carefully taught the kids aged eight to twelve how to do it. Soon, he was leading teams working on four docks, with twenty boats bringing in piles of fish each day.

"All the kids were thrilled with the project. They enjoyed working together and were having great fun. They were contributing to the good of the village. Ariel was especially happy for Micah. He had become an important member of the group.

"More and more, the villagers came to appreciate Ariel's ability as a leader. He was constantly developing ideas for bigger projects and activities. But no one could have imagined the magnitude of a dream he was having for a project influenced by the mysterious happenings he had heard were occurring in and around the region."

CHAPTER 7

MYSTERIOUS
HAPPENINGS

ONE EVENING, MICAH'S uncles discussed sightings
in the region of a popular new rabbi named Jesus of
Nazareth. He had been raised as a carpenter but had grown to
be a gifted spiritual teacher. In just two years, he had proven
to be much different than any of the other rabbis or prophets
who traveled the area. He was a master of the Scriptures. He
had preached amazing sermons, including one people now call
'the Sermon on the Mount.' People came from miles to hear
him preach. He had selected twelve men to be his disciples.
Interestingly, these men were not spiritual leaders but were
common folk. Four were fishermen and one was even a tax
collector. But there was more.

"'It is said that Jesus has even claimed to be the Messiah!'
Daniel reported. 'He was reading the Scriptures in a synagogue in
his hometown and told the people he had fulfilled that prophecy.'

"Naomi, Joshua, and Benjamin gasped and asked how the
crowd had reacted. 'These were people who had known him since

birth,' Daniel replied. 'To them, he was just one of the village kids who had grown to adulthood. They were horrified that he would say such a thing. Many started yelling 'blasphemy'—the penalty for which is death. The crowd scrambled to capture him and kill him. They shoved him toward a cliff, but, miraculously, he escaped through the crowd. Now he lives and often preaches near here. But there is more.'

"The light from the fireplace lit up Daniel's face. 'This rabbi has performed astounding miracles. He has healed people of leprosy. He told a lame man to get up and walk. He healed a Roman centurion's dying servant without even seeing him! He made a blind man see. One report is that he even walked on water and calmed raging storms right here on the Sea of Galilee!'

"'But you haven't heard the best part yet,' Daniel continued. 'On more than one occasion, he has raised a person from the dead!'

"Everyone's eyes grew big. 'How could this be?' they asked.

"Daniel's tone grew solemn. 'Jesus preaches the importance of faith in God. He says everything is possible for those who believe. He has scolded his own disciples for their lack of faith. He has even scolded the priests for theirs. He talks about the blessedness of simple people who have no earthly riches but have strong faith.'

"Daniel looked around the room. 'Just today, Ariel discussed an interesting idea with me. The kids' fishing project has been a success, and he thinks it would be good to plan an even greater project. Jesus travels in and out of Capernaum several times a year. Ariel asked if he and the village kids could take Micah to see him the next time he comes. Maybe he could heal Micah.'

"Naomi's heart leaped when she heard Ariel's proposal. Then she shrank in fear. Of course, Micah being healed would be the answer to all her prayers. But what if the stories about Jesus weren't true? What if this rabbi was one of the false prophets about whom the Scriptures warned? Micah would not be able to handle such a disappointment. His and Naomi's hearts—and the hearts of all around them—would be forever broken. Their faith in God would be shattered. What would she do afterward to take care of him?

"The risk was huge. Naomi buried her face in her hands.

"That night, Naomi went into a deep sleep. In a dream, she saw Jesus walking along the Sea of Galilee. Micah was walking alongside him, just like any other man. She saw her husband, Caleb, approach Micah and give him a warm embrace. There were smiles on the faces of Micah's family and friends who had given their love and support to him all these years.

"Naomi awoke with renewed faith and greater excitement than when she had been a young girl. She awakened Micah to tell him she would be gone that morning but would return by noon. She hurried from her little house and went down the dirt road toward the Sea of Galilee. Weaving through the people by the roadside markets, she soon came to the shore where Daniel, Joshua, and Benjamin kept their boats.

"Calling the uncles together, she told them about her dream. She was ready to take Micah to see the rabbi. If Jesus truly performed miracles, Micah would walk, and his life would be forever changed. More important, his faith would be rewarded, and so would the faith of the whole village after seeing such a miracle.

"The uncles wanted to pray about it. They told her they would come to see her when they felt God had given them guidance.

"On Friday evening, the uncles gathered at Naomi's house. They waited until Micah was asleep. One by one, they revealed that their prayers had led them to the same conclusion. This was truly Micah's chance of a lifetime. The evidence was strong that Jesus was the Messiah. Another lifetime test of faith was before them. They couldn't fail Micah or Naomi, and, especially, God. Their next actions had to be clear and bold."

CHAPTER 8

MICAH FALTERS

A S DANIEL AND Ariel made their plans, they learned that Jesus would be in Capernaum in two weeks. The family decided to wait until the last day before Jesus' arrival to tell Micah.

"When they told him, he turned pale. This presented gut-wrenching problems. What if it didn't work? Should he even get his hopes up? Even more frightening, no one knew how much he doubted God. He not only distrusted God's love, but he had also denied his very existence. If there was a God, Micah was afraid to face him. He was afraid that Jesus would recognize him as a sinner and reject him before his family and the people in the village. Too many lives would be permanently damaged.

"Micah called for his grandfather. 'Grandfather,' he said, 'I cannot do this.' Grandfather listened intently as Micah explained. His doubts sounded like those of dozens of people described in the Scriptures.

"Grandfather took him by the shoulders. 'Micah, you are no different than the great kings of Israel,' he said. 'Think of the stories of Moses and Abraham. Abraham laughed when God told him Sarah would have a child at age ninety. Moses argued with God at the burning bush. Saul, David, and Solomon disappointed God when they became terrible sinners. The prophets told the kings what I'm going to tell you: trust God. Have faith in God. While you may have strayed away from him, he has never strayed from you.'

"Micah wept, and Grandfather took him in his arms. The next morning would be the biggest day of everyone's life."

CHAPTER 9

It's Time

EARLY THE NEXT morning, the entire village turned out to participate in this amazing event. Ariel and Micah's uncles gathered the kids in the village, and Ariel explained what they could do if they all worked together. The uncles would carry Micah on a cart to where Jesus was. All the young people would follow along behind.

"Some asked what would happen if Micah wasn't healed. Ariel replied that the evidence was too strong that Jesus was who he claimed to be. He also argued that they would not want to miss seeing the miracle of Jesus healing Micah. Almost everyone was excited, but a few were not so sure.

"'Micah is not our responsibility,' one boy said. 'Shouldn't his family take care of this?'

"'He is our friend and our neighbor,' Ariel replied. 'He'd do it for any one of us. We should all want to be part of something this wonderful.'

"Ariel was a strong leader, and Micah was his friend and part of the group. In the end, no one wanted to be left out. So they lifted Micah into the back of the cart. Together, the group, along with Micah's family, pulled and pushed the cart down the dirt road. They came to a hill overlooking the small, mud brick house where the rabbi was speaking. A crowd had gathered outside, and a line of people stood at the door.

"The group pulled Micah's cart to the edge of the crowd. Everyone was quiet. They strained to hear the rabbi's voice. He spoke of loving God and loving one another. He talked about seeking God's kingdom first, and that all other things would flow from that. Finally, he spoke of the importance of faith.

"The line of people began to slowly move. The house was completely filled, and it was not possible to see what was happening inside. The crowd outside was anxious and moved closer. Arguments broke out. The rabbi's disciples came out to try and quiet them.

"As the day wore on, the hot sun, dust, and lack of food and water took their toll on the crowd. Those who had no personal concerns for Jesus to address left as the rabbi finished preaching. Those with doubts and no real faith left as well.

"The sun was sinking low in the sky. The inside of the house was still crowded. No one made way for those who had special needs. Hope for anyone like Micah was slipping away as the late afternoon shadows began to appear.

"'Can you make way for our nephew?' Micah's uncles began asking those in line. 'He is disabled, and this may be his only chance to be healed.'

"Those on the outer edges of the crowd showed little sympathy. 'Friend,' said one man, 'there is only one of him and many of those like your nephew. Time may run out before he can be seen by the rabbi.'

"Micah's uncles gathered to talk. So much had led up to this day. It had been so hard to get Micah here. Jesus might leave, and Micah's opportunity might not come again.

"Grandfather saw a narrow stairway leading to the roof of the house. Roofs had special importance. They provided people with a place to sleep outside where it was cooler than inside during the summer months. Grandfather told the uncles they must carry Micah to the roof.

"'But, what then?' everyone asked. 'There is no entry to the house from the roof.'

"'Then we'll break through the roof!' Grandfather exclaimed. 'We have come too far to be denied.'

"The uncles were amazed, but there was no time to argue. The men moved quickly and picked up Micah from the cart. He was so hot and tired he couldn't move. The mat on which he was lying provided the support his uncles needed to carry him. They wrapped it around him to keep him straight so he would fit up the narrow stairway.

"Once on the roof, the uncles quickly decided on the best spot to chop a hole. They guessed that Jesus might be to one side of the room below, so they thought the center would be best. Grandfather brought a hammer and an ax, and the group began to chop through the roof, which was made of wooden beams covered cross-wise with straw cemented together with mud.

IT'S TIME

"Immediately, people came running up the stairs to find out the cause of the commotion. The owner of the house pushed Micah's uncles away from the damage they were doing. But already a few blows had caused a large piece of the fragile roof to cave in. Everyone rushed over to look down into the dimly-lit room. They saw, gazing up at them, the face of a man."

CHAPTER 10

THE RABBI

THE MAN'S HAIR was covered with a light layer of dust and particles from the damaged roof. He waved his hand for the uncles to complete their work. He smiled when the uncles grabbed the corners of a mat and began lowering a young man down into the house. Men from inside reached up to help lower Micah to the floor in front of the rabbi.

"Micah now lay on his back. As he looked up, he saw a circle of faces straining to see him. Some seemed annoyed—even angry—at this intrusion. Others simply stared at him. The rabbi stood straight with his hands to his sides and looked down at Micah. Micah had the strangest sensation that he knew this man, and had known him always.

"For some reason, Micah began talking, though the rabbi had not yet said anything to him. 'Oh, sweet Lord, thank you for seeing me. God has breathed life into me. For reasons known only to him, he has made me unable to walk. But he has also given me many blessings. He has given me a wonderful mother,

51

grandfather, and uncles who love me more than their own lives. He has seen me through the toughest times. He has given me the friendship of an entire village. Now he has fulfilled the prophecies by sending you. I am looking at you, and feel that I am seeing the face of God.'

"'But I have been weak, oh Lord,' Micah continued. 'The torments of my life have taken away my faith. I have sinned mightily by forsaking God, by doubting his existence, and, yes, even by cursing him. I am not worthy, Lord Jesus. My whole village has carried me, physically and spiritually, to come see you in the hope that you might heal me. I am greatly ashamed of my sins. No matter what happens today, I hope that you will have mercy on me.'

"Everyone in the room was amazed at this confession of sin. Jesus continued to softly smile, but his eyes had welled up with tears. He had seen the faith of Micah's group from the very start. Slowly, he lifted his eyes upward to where he could see the sky through the hole in the roof. He kept them there for quite some time. Not a person in the room made the slightest sound. Micah felt more at peace than he had in his entire life.

"Jesus lowered his eyes down to meet Micah's. 'Son, your sins are forgiven,' he said. 'Take up your mat and go home.'

"Some of the scribes were there, and they asked themselves, 'Why does this man speak this way? He is blaspheming! Who but God alone can forgive sins?'

"Jesus immediately knew what they were thinking. 'Why are you thinking such things in your hearts?' he said. 'Which is easier: to say to the disabled person, "Your sins are forgiven," or to say, "Rise, pick up your mat, and walk"? But that you may know the Son of Man has authority to forgive sins on earth, I say to this man, "Rise, pick up your mat, and go home."'

"Micah was bewildered. He looked around at the men who were staring down at him. In all his life he had never had feeling, much less strength, in his legs. However, he slowly began to pull his knees up beneath him. He put one foot on the floor, then slowly pushed his way up straight until he could put the other foot next to it. Finally, he was able to stand as steadily as anyone else.

"Everyone stood back in amazement. Many placed their hands over their mouths or put both hands up to the sides of their faces. Then Jesus motioned for Micah to come to him. Micah took one step, then two, and Jesus took him in his arms.

"'Truly, I have never witnessed anything like this!' someone said. Voices began to erupt throughout the room. Micah's grandfather and uncles wept openly.

"Micah backed away from Jesus and slowly lowered himself to where he could pick up his mat. He turned toward the door and walked toward the light where he knew who would be waiting."

CHAPTER 11

FAITH REWARDED

A S MICAH REACHED the door, he saw the group who had supported him. The whole village was there. Ariel stood in front with the young people. His friend put his arms around him, and everyone laughed and cheered at the top of their lungs.

"The crowd parted, and there was Micah's mother. She covered her mouth with both hands and wept out loud. She moved quickly to him and took him in her arms. As the crowd gathered around them, they embraced for a long time. The burden of years of misery was lifting. Everyone continued to cheer and praise God.

A Miracle for Micah

"Micah, his family, and his friends left the house and walked to a hillside overlooking Capernaum. For the most part they stood in silence and prayed, still marveling at what they had just experienced. Then, down the hill, they saw Jesus appear from the house and walk toward the lake, still preaching to all who followed along.

"Words could not express what everyone was thinking. What had happened was beyond anything they could understand. All they knew was their amazement, their gratitude, and now their renewed and unshakable faith in God. Finally, they turned toward home.

"But who could have guessed that God's purpose for Micah's life was just beginning?"

CHAPTER 12

A Warrior at Last

THE MAN GOT up to stir the fire.

"Whatever happened to Micah?" Reuben asked. He was now sitting in the middle of the bed.

"Oh, he's hard at work," the man replied. "God has placed many people in his life. He has gone on to share his experiences and lessons with people of all ages who have suffered hard times. There are so many. You have suffered from a physical disability. Others have been sick, or lost their jobs, or had a family member die, or watched their family break up, or experienced failure of some other type. Each of these causes pain, fear, anxiety, anger, loneliness, and lack of hope.

"It is often difficult for these individuals to find comfort and support. People who haven't experienced these things are unable to understand. Many times, they make things worse through their lack of sympathy or by avoiding, slandering, taunting, or even bullying the person.

"That is where faith in God becomes the most important source of comfort. Jesus taught us to love God and love one another. All of God's creations are made for a purpose. Love means we respect and learn from one another as God molds us into what he wants us to be. Hard times are conquered through faith.

"Micah had seen so much misery. But through his life, God healed an individual, a family, and a whole village. And who knows the impact his healing had on the crowd who stood there that day so many years ago? Had Micah been born with an able body, we might never have seen all these healings and learned the lessons they teach."

"Where is Micah today?" Reuben asked.

"Oh, people see him all the time," the man answered. "They remember the disabled child whom they didn't know, understand, or appreciate. Today, he has many friends, and they all help him."

"It's too bad he couldn't have gone on to be the warrior his parents wanted him to be," said Reuben.

"But he did," replied the man. "He's a warrior for Jesus. The Zealots worked to defeat the Romans and those of ungodly faith through military methods. But Jesus modeled love for God and for one another and the hope that brings. He taught us to trust in God's wisdom and not our own. He advised that the one who believes in him would also do the works he did. He assured us that our faith will be rewarded, and he has gone to prepare a place for us in his father's house.

"Like many of the Zealots, Jesus died for his beliefs. But the major difference is that he conquered death and rose to live again, which proved that he truly is the Son of God. Micah carries Jesus' word to everyone he meets through his life and deeds. Jesus' warriors are winning far greater victories than the Zealots. We can all be warriors for Jesus if we choose to be."

The man patted Reuben on the shoulder. "Now that you know of Micah and his story, perhaps you will see how you can be one of Jesus' warriors, too."

A knock on the door interrupted their talk. The man went and opened it, and Reuben's mother and father stepped quickly into the tiny room. They glanced at the man, and then saw Reuben on the bed. They rushed to gather him into their arms. All of them cried as Reuben's parents told him how worried they had been, how happy they were to find him, and most important, how much they loved him.

The man left the room to let them be alone. Soon, they came to tell him goodbye. They shook his hand as he rubbed Reuben's head.

Reuben's father could no longer hold back tears. "Thank you, Micah," he said. "You have done the Lord's work once again. This time it was for us. May God bless you as you continue to do his work."

Reuben was astonished! The man was Micah! Reuben realized he had been rescued by the once-disabled child who had actually seen the face of Jesus and been healed by him.

Micah smiled. "As you said, it is the Lord's work. It is through each of us and for all of us that he does what he does. We must pass on our lessons to as many as we can. Young Reuben has a wonderful life ahead. He only needs to keep his faith in hard times and trust in God's wisdom. We hope to live long to see God's plan for him unfold."

INSPIRATIONS

THIS STORY WAS inspired by the true life of a young man who has been disabled since birth. It is reflective of the following Bible verses.

"For I know the plans I have for you," declares the LORD, "plans to prosper you and not to harm you, plans to give you hope and a future. Then you will call upon me and come and pray to me, and I will listen to you. You will seek me and find me when you seek me with all your heart."
—Jeremiah 29:11-13

I tell you the truth, anyone who has faith in me will do what I have been doing. He will do even greater things than these, because I am going to the Father.
—John 14:12

A MIRACLE FOR MICAH

Trust in the LORD with all your heart and lean not on your own understanding; in all your ways acknowledge him, and he will make your paths straight.

—Proverbs 3:5-6

One of them, an expert in the law, tested him with this question: "Teacher, which is the greatest commandment in the Law?" Jesus replied: "'Love the Lord your God with all your heart and with all your soul and with all your mind.' This is the first and greatest commandment. And the second is like it: 'Love your neighbor as yourself.' All the Law and the Prophets hang on these two commandments."

—Matthew 22:35-40

A few days later, when Jesus again entered Capernaum, the people heard that he had come home. So many gathered that there was no room left, not even outside the door, and he preached the word to them. Some men came, bringing to him a disabled person, carried by four of them. Since they could not get him to Jesus because of the crowd, they made an opening in the roof above Jesus and, after digging through it, lowered the mat the disabled man was lying on. When Jesus saw their faith, he said to the disabled man, "Son, your sins are forgiven."

Now some teachers of the law were sitting there, thinking to themselves, "Why does this fellow talk like that? He's blaspheming! Who can forgive sins but God alone?"

Immediately Jesus knew in his spirit that this was what they were thinking in their hearts, and he said to them, "Why are you thinking these things? Which is easier: to say to the disabled man, 'Your sins are forgiven,' or to say, 'Get up, take your mat and walk'? But that you may know that the Son of Man has authority on earth to forgive sins ..." He said to the disabled man, "I tell you, get up, take your mat and go home." He got up, took his mat and walked out in full view of them all. This amazed everyone and they praised God, saying, "We have never seen anything like this!"

—Mark 2:1-12

"If you can?" said Jesus. "Everything is possible for him who believes."

—Mark 9:23

Look to the LORD and his strength; seek his face always.

—1 Chronicles 16:11

Do not let your hearts be troubled. Trust in God; trust also in me. In my Father's house are many rooms; if it were not so, I would have told you. I am going there to prepare a place for you. And if I go and prepare a place for you, I will come back and take you to be with me that you also may be where I am.

—John 14:1-3

DISCUSSION GUIDE

T HE FOLLOWING DISCUSSION questions are for use with *A Miracle for Micah*. Young people can use them individually or in group discussions, and they can also be used as homework assignments for Sunday school or homeschool students. The questions will encourage discussions among friends, family members, and teachers. We hope you enjoyed reading *A Miracle for Micah* and that you will use these questions to talk about the ideas presented in the book.

Chapter 1: Escape
1. What did you think about Reuben's situation?
2. Have you ever had a situation in which you felt desperate?
3. What kinds of situations would make a person feel desperate?
4. Who could you or others turn to for advice and comfort?

5. What would keep you from turning to someone for advice and comfort?
6. What actions should you take before developing a plan of your own to deal with a situation?

Chapter 2: From Warriors He Came

1. Have you ever known or observed natural leaders in your group, school, church, or community?
2. How would you describe them?
3. What effect have such leaders had on you?
4. Have you ever known leaders who had bad effects on you or other people?
5. How do you react to good and bad leaders?

Chapter 3: Terrible and Unfair

1. Have you ever had terrible and unfair situations affect you, your family, or your friends?
2. What kinds of situations were they (sickness, death, loss of job, family breakups, relocation to new neighborhoods, schools, or towns)?
3. What effect did those situations have on you and others involved?
4. How did people cope with these situations?
5. Was there a particular leader who everyone relied on for guidance, advice, or comfort?
6. Have you ever prayed about such situations?

Chapter 4: The Blessing of Young People

1. Have you ever thought of the young kids with whom you associate as being the future of your community?
2. How does this make you think about these kids' education, behavior, and the activities in which they are involved?

3. Who are the leaders in your age group?
4. Are there negative leaders?
5. What effects do positive and negative leaders have on you and those around you?
6. Are there kids in your age group who are left out of activities? If so, why?
7. How do you see yourself in your age group?
8. How does this affect you?

Chapter 5: A Family's Wisdom
1. Does your family meet regularly in some setting to talk to one another?
2. If so, what types of settings?
3. What kinds of conversations do you have?
4. What do you learn through such conversations?
5. Are you able to share your personal activities, triumphs, concerns, worries, and questions with your family?
6. Do you think such conversations are important sources of advice, comfort, solutions, or answers?

Chapter 6: Ariel's Great Idea
1. Do you see yourself as a leader? If not, do you still see opportunities to make great contributions?
2. What ideas do you have for contributions in your community?
3. How would you go about making those ideas happen?
4. With whom could you share your ideas?

Chapter 7: Mysterious Happenings
1. Have you ever dreamed about being involved in some major contribution, activity, or project if given the chance?

2. What might those be?
3. Who could you go to with your idea?
4. How would you present it?
5. Who could join with you to present the idea?
6. What effects could you have on your community, school, or church if you were successful?

Chapter 8: Micah Falters
1. Have you ever had a great idea, but then had second thoughts or doubts before you presented it?
2. What caused you to have these doubts or second thoughts?
3. How hard is it to convince friends, parents, teachers, or even bullies that you have a great idea?
4. What are the risks of presenting what you feel is a great idea? What are the rewards?
5. To whom can you go for advice and encouragement to help you develop and "sell" your ideas?

Chapter 9: It's Time
1. Have you ever hesitated to bring up an idea you had, only to have someone else bring it up?
2. How did you feel after you hesitated and someone else got credit for your idea?
3. What caused you to hesitate?
4. What actions should you take to ensure your idea is good, well thought out, and beneficial?
5. When is it time to act?
6. What might happen in the future if you do or don't take action?

DISCUSSION GUIDE

Chapter 10: The Rabbi
1. What do you think is meant by the statement, "Micah had the strangest sensation that he knew this man, and had known him always"?
2. Have you ever followed through with an idea to its completion and seen amazing results? If so, what results did you see?
3. Have you ever seen someone in your school, church, or other organization follow through with an idea to completion? If so, what happened?
4. Who were the main contributors to the success of the idea?
5. Has this experience given you skill and confidence to take on bigger projects?

Chapter 11: Faith Rewarded
1. What was the impact on everyone involved when the idea was put into action?
2. Have you ever thought back on what might have stopped you from seeing the idea through to completion?
3. If so, what gave everyone the courage to go on?
4. Have you ever thought about what would have happened if you had given up?
5. How have you, your group, community, or some individual benefitted from a great idea?

Chapter 12: A Warrior at Last
1. Who in your group, school, church, or community are leaders even though they don't fit the usual physical, mental, or social mold of what people expect leaders to be like?

2. Have you ever known, heard of, read about, or even seen in movies or television amazing people who have influenced others through their efforts, ideas, skills, or reactions to hard times?
3. Do you know any "unlikely leaders"—those whom you never thought would have been able to influence others?
4. How did these people influence others?
5. What personal characteristics, behaviors, or teaching methods caused Jesus to be such an influential leader?
6. Micah was an unlikely leader. How did Jesus influence him to carry on his work?
7. What influence is Jesus having on you?
8. What work might he have you do?

WinePress Kids
Great Books, Defined.

To order additional copies of this book call:
1-877-421-READ (7323)
or please visit our website at
www.WinePressbooks.com

If you enjoyed this quality custom-published book,
drop by our website for more books and information.

www.winepresspublishing.com
"Your partner in custom publishing."

CPSIA information can be obtained at www.ICGtesting.com
Printed in the USA
LVOW13s1019120713

342522LV00006B/14/P